Arnold Sundgaard THE LAMB
AND THE BUTTERFLY

Pictures by Eric Carle

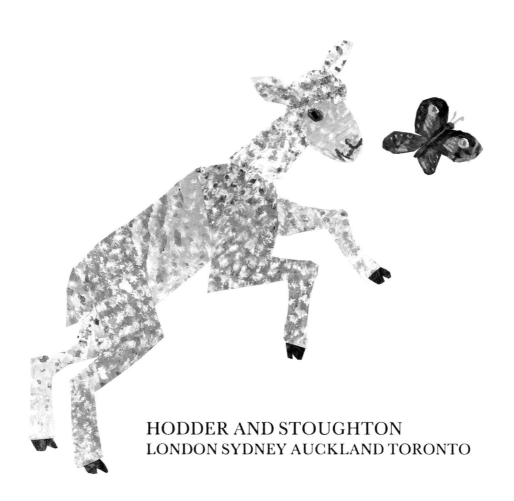

HODDER AND STOUGHTON
LONDON SYDNEY AUCKLAND TORONTO

A Lamb and a Butterfly
met one day
in the middle of a meadow.
The Lamb asked the Butterfly,
"Where is your mother?"
The Butterfly answered,
"I haven't the slightest idea.
My mother flies one way
while I fly another."

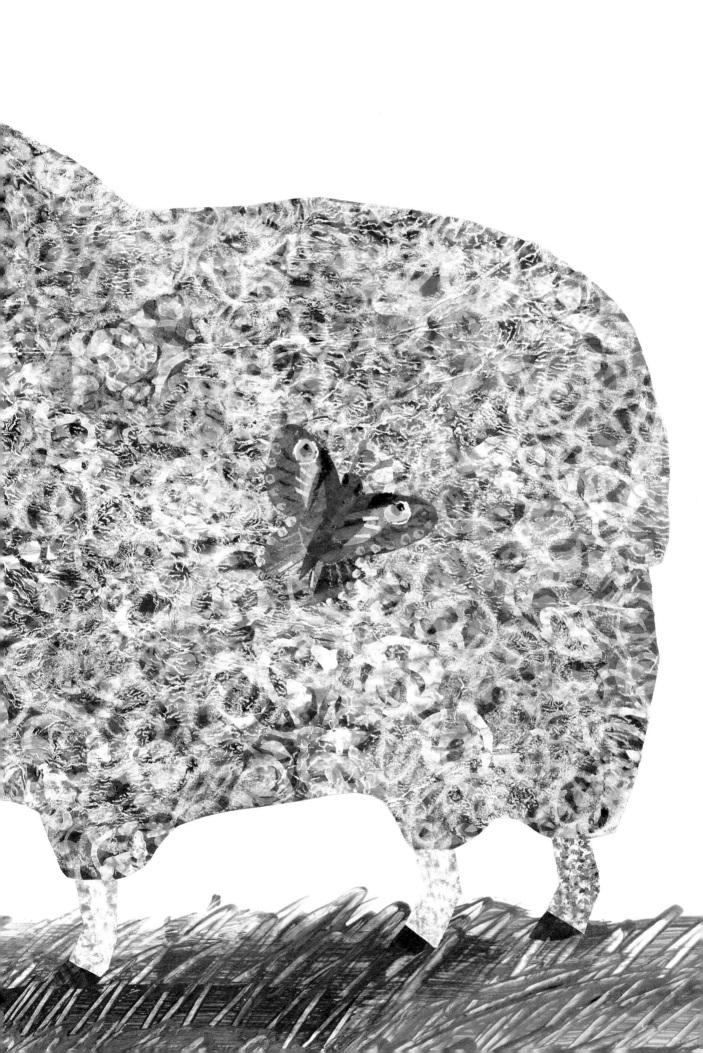

And with a zig and a zag,
and a ziggety zag,
the Butterfly fluttered away
and landed on a dandelion.
The Lamb kicked up her heels
and ran after him.
"Where is your home?"
the Lamb asked the Butterfly.
"The world is my home,"
answered the Butterfly.
"I am free to fly anywhere."

And with a zig and a zag,
and a ziggety zag,
the Butterfly fluttered away
and landed on a bristle thistle.
The Lamb kicked up her heels
and ran after him.
"But where do you sleep?"
the Lamb asked the Butterfly.
"I sleep where I please,"
said the Butterfly to the Lamb.
"Wherever I am,
well, that's where I sleep."

And with a zig and a zag,
and a ziggety zag,
the Butterfly fluttered away
and landed on a poppy.
The Lamb kicked up her heels
and ran after him.
"Why do you flutter so?"
the Lamb asked the Butterfly.
"Why shouldn't I flutter?"
the Butterfly asked in reply.
"Well, lambs don't flutter,"
said the Lamb to the Butterfly.
"We walk in a straight line.
One follows the other."
"But I don't follow anyone,"
said the Butterfly to the Lamb.
"I go wherever I choose.
And now I choose to leave this meadow."

And with a zig and a zag,
and a ziggety zag,
the Butterfly left the meadow
and landed on a sunflower.
The Lamb ran after him.
"Come back, come back," she cried,
"I want to ask you a question."
"What is your question?"
the Butterfly asked the Lamb.
"Please don't leave me,"
the Lamb implored the Butterfly.
"That's not a question,"
said the Butterfly to the Lamb.
"Put it in the form of a question."
And the Lamb said,
"Why don't you stay with me?
My mother will take care of you."

With a zig and a zag,
and a ziggety zag,
the Butterfly flew into the sky.
"I don't need anyone
to take care of me,"
said the Butterfly to the Lamb.
"I'm on my way," he cried.
"Good-bye! Good-bye!"

But at that very moment
a fierce, black cloud
darkened the sky,
and rain began to fall.
An angry gust of wind
caught the Butterfly's wings
and he was swept out of sight.
Then the Lamb
heard her mother bleating,
and she hurried to her side.
"What were you doing
at the far end of the meadow?"
the mother asked the Lamb.
"I followed a Butterfly,"
said the Lamb to her mother,
"and now he is lost in the storm."
"Poor Butterfly,"
said the mother to the Lamb,
"but that's what happens
when you go fluttering
this way and that."

"But now I will never see him again,"
said the Lamb to her mother.
"He is gone forever."
And then the mother asked,
"What is that on your back?"
"What is what on my back?"
the Lamb asked her mother.
"Isn't that a butterfly?"
the mother asked the Lamb.
And she was right.
Sure enough,
there on the back of the Lamb
was the Butterfly himself.
His wings were wet and bedraggled.
He looked as though
he would never fly again.
"Now will you stay?"
the Lamb asked the Butterfly.
"Let me think about it,"
said the Butterfly to the Lamb,
as he dried out his wings.

By now the sun had come out.
Slowly the Butterfly tried to flutter.
With a zig, zig, zig,
and a zag, zag, zag,
and a ziggety, ziggety zig zag,
he managed to reach a honeysuckle vine.
In one of its blossoms
he found a pool of nectar.
And he sipped and he sipped and he sipped
until he felt strong again.
"What have you decided?"
the Lamb asked the Butterfly.
"I'd like to stay,"
said the Butterfly to the Lamb,
"but I really must be on my way.
I'm heading south, you know."
"But why go south?" cried the Lamb.
"Because I don't have a woolly coat like yours
to keep me warm.
If I stayed here I'd freeze."

"Well, if that is so,"
said the Lamb to the Butterfly,
"I won't try to stop you."
"Please don't think me ungrateful,"
said the Butterfly to the Lamb.
And spreading his wings
in the splendid act of flight,
he zigged and he zagged
and he ziggety zagged,
and soon was lost from sight.

This time the Lamb
did not kick up her heels
and run after him.
She walked instead to her mother's side,
and never asked a Butterfly
to join a flock of sheep again.

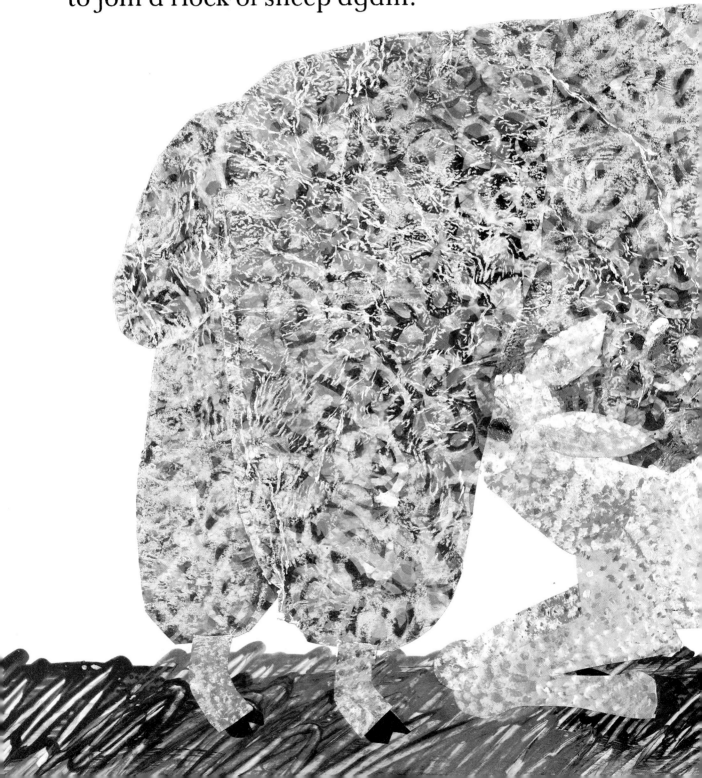

Arnold Sundgaard

is a playwright, librettist, and author who has won many awards and prizes for his writings, including a Rockefeller Fellowship in Drama and a Guggenheim Fellowship for Creative Writing. Among his many well-known works are the opera *Down in the Valley*, with music by Kurt Weill; *The Lowland Sea*, with music by Alec Wilder; and a new opera, *Mosaic*, with music by Fabian Watkinson, first performed in London in March, 1988. He has also collaborated on a number of works for children, including *Young Abe Lincoln*, with music by Victor Ziskin. Recently he has turned his lyrical talents to the writing of books for children.

The inspiration for *The Lamb and the Butterfly* came, he says, from his long-time interest in the miracle of the migratory flight of both birds and butterflies. Why do these creatures make these incredible journeys? How do they know where and when to go? "I thought a lamb, who never leaves her mother's side, might ask the questions for me," he said.

Born in Minnesota, Mr Sundgaard now lives in Massachusetts, USA.

Eric Carle

is known around the world for his many highly original and beautiful picture books. Born in Syracuse, New York, he lived for a number of years in Germany and received his art training there. Returning to the United States, he worked as an art director for a large advertising agency before deciding to devote his full time to creating books for children. The first book he both wrote and illustrated was a counting book, *1, 2, 3 to the Zoo*, which was an immediate and lasting success. This was followed by his *The Very Hungry Caterpillar*, an immensely popular book that has become a modern classic and has been translated into more than a dozen languages. Among his more recent works are *Papa, please get the moon for me, The Greedy Python and The Foolish Tortoise, The Tiny Seed, Have You Seen My Cat?* and *A House for Hermit Crab*.

Since his early childhood, Eric Carle has been intensely interested in nature, and many of his books have animals or insects as characters. Butterflies, in particular, symbolise for him the spirit of artistic creation, and they appear in nearly all his works. The pictures for this book are done in a combination of acrylic painting and collage. The papers used in the collages are first painted by Mr Carle, then cut out and intricately layered to produce very subtle textural effects.

Eric Carle and his wife live in Massachusetts, USA.

British Library Cataloguing in Publication Data

Sundgaard, Arnold
    The lamb and the butterfly.
    I. Title   II. Carle, Eric, *1929-*
    823'.914 [J]

    ISBN 0-340-49580-4

Text copyright © Arnold Sundgaard 1988
Illustrations copyright © Eric Carle Corporation 1988

First published 1988 by Orchard Books, USA
First published in Great Britain 1989

Published by Hodder and Stoughton Children's Books,
a division of Hodder and Stoughton Ltd,
Mill Road, Dunton Green, Sevenoaks, Kent TN13 2YJ

Printed in USA

Book design by Jean Krulis and Eric Carle

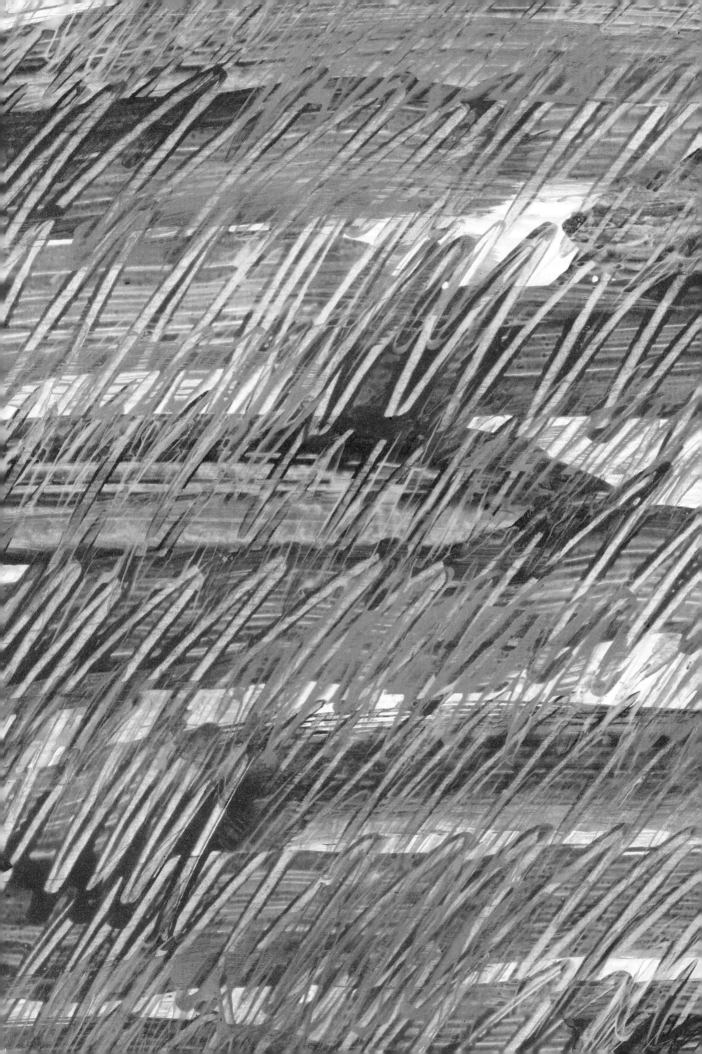